BABAR
LEARNS TO COOK

A Random House PICTUREBACK®

Laurent de Brunhoff

Random House 🏠 New York

BABAR
LEARNS TO COOK

Library of Congress Cataloging in Publication Data: Brunhoff, Laurent de. Babar learns to cook. SUMMARY: After Babar and Celeste watch him on television, Truffles, the most famous chef in Celesteville, comes to the palace to give cooking lessons. [1. Elephants—Fiction. 2. Cookery—Fiction] I. Title. PZ7.B82843Baal [E] 78-11769. ISBN: 0-394-84107-7 (B.C.); 0-394-84108-5 (trade); 0-394-94108-X (lib. bdg.).

Babar, the elephant king, and Queen Celeste are watching television with Cousin Arthur and their friend the Old Lady. Truffles, the most famous chef in Celesteville, is giving a cooking lesson.

"Isn't he great?" says Flora.

Celeste decides to call Chef Truffles on the telephone.
"Will you come to the palace and teach us some of your
marvelous recipes?" she asks.

"I'd be delighted," answers the chef.

When Chef Truffles arrives at the palace, Pom, Flora, and
Alexander rush outside with their mother to greet him.
"Are you going to make us some cakes?" they ask.

The chef rolls up his sleeves, ties on an apron, and puts his chef's hat on his head. Now he is ready for his first cooking lesson. Flora wishes she had a chef's hat, too.

Chef Truffles' cooking class has gathered in the palace kitchen. All of his students watch very closely and listen quietly.

For his first lesson, the chef is making stuffed mushrooms. While he prepares the stuffing, he tells the class how to do what he is doing. Babar is fascinated.

The stuffing is almost ready. The chef tastes it with a swift dip of his trunk.

"Would you like me to put in a little more butter?" asks Cousin Arthur.

At last the stuffed mushrooms are taken out of the oven. Everybody admires their golden-brown color. Rushing up to snap a picture, one of the students exclaims, "What a delicious-looking dish!"

When the lesson is over, every student in the class gets a plate with a stuffed mushroom. "This is excellent!" says Babar. "Congratulations, Chef Truffles!"

Arthur is passing the tray around. "Who doesn't have a plate?" he asks.

"I don't!" cries Alexander.

"That's not true," says Flora. "You already ate your stuffed mushroom!" The two children start to fight.

"Watch out!" cries Arthur. In the scuffle, he drops the tray. . . .

Queen Celeste is very upset.
The chef is furious! "Children!" he
grumbles. "Always getting into trouble!"

Chef Truffles orders
the children to leave.
Pom and Arthur tell
Flora and Alexander
that it's all their fault.

Later that day the chef takes a nap in the palace garden.
The children creep up and start to giggle because he is snoring
so loudly. All of a sudden, Alexander snatches the chef's hat.

Arthur grabs it. "I'm the chef, now!" he says, putting the hat on his head.

"Arthur is the chef! Arthur is the chef!" sing Pom, Flora, and Alexander.

The children decide to have a cooking class of their own.
While Arthur very seriously stirs a chocolate sauce, the little
ones are busy slicing cucumbers. The slicing machine is fun.

But making cucumber soup with the mixer is even better! Then they decide to make cucumber juice. They are so excited that Pom starts the blender before Flora can put on the top! . . .

The children quickly try to hide the results of their cooking lesson. But Celeste catches them. "You little rascals," she scolds. "What if the chef should come in and see this messy kitchen?"

Queen Celeste helps the children clean up the mess.
Arthur pretends he had nothing to do with it. He asks
the queen to taste his chocolate sauce. It is delicious!

Meanwhile Chef Truffles has awakened. "Someone has stolen
my hat!" he screams as he crawls around on the ground.
Arthur brings back the hat, covered with cucumber stains.

Outraged, Chef Truffles calls him a little imp. Then
Celeste hurries over and makes him taste Arthur's sauce.
"Why, it's excellent," declares the chef with a smile.

Chef Truffles bakes a cake to go with Arthur's chocolate sauce. But when he pours the sauce out of the pot, some of it lands on Pom's head. Nobody is perfect. . . .

Celeste wipes off the sauce.
"Now it's my turn to cook,"
she says. "I'm going to make
a strawberry soufflé."

The children hurry out to the garden and pick a basketful
of strawberries. Of course, they can't help eating a few.
Fresh strawberries taste so good!

Celeste whips the egg whites. Flora arrives just in time
with the basket of strawberries.

"I love strawberry soufflé," says Babar. "Make it a big one!"

Everyone sits down at the table, including Chef Truffles. They are eager to taste Celeste's soufflé and the cake with Arthur's chocolate sauce.

"We had better start with the strawberry soufflé before it collapses," says Chef Truffles. Celeste gives everyone a big helping. Then Babar has two slices of the cake. What a feast!

Chef Truffles is proud of his students. Now that the cooking lessons are over, he gives everyone an award. Each boy receives a nice white chef's hat, and each girl gets a blue ribbon and medal.

But Flora is not happy. "It's not fair!" she says. "I want a white hat, too!"

"Flora is right," says Celeste. "We should all get hats."

Babar agrees with Celeste and Flora. So the chef gives hats to everyone, except the Old Lady. She doesn't think that she would look good in a chef's hat.

52656

E
Brunhoff

Brunhoff, Laurent
Babar learns to
cook

DATE DUE

AUG 2 0 2001	JUN 3 2011
JUN 1 1 2003	JUL 0 7 2012
AUG 3 0 2003	JUL 2 7 2012
AUG 2 6 2004	APR 5 8 2014
TRoy 12-17	OCT 0 7 2016
NOV 2 4 2005	MAR 2 2020
2008	
COE 1-11-2018